S0-BYN-155

Projects NB

Spain projects due 20th
Desert island lists

Reminders

Pet + Produce Day practices
Lamb Calling - after school
    Thurs - Mrs Goulding

Lady Robinson Sewing Basket
entries - Fri - lunch time
    Mrs Lopdell

AGENDA FOR
GRANDPARENTS DAY

Kapa Haka, Mā'ulu'ulu

---

lotus
dog u

QUIET

JAKE H
CARLA
BILLY
LOLLY

MUS

Tuba

Violi

dog

LUE

Carla - Tu

Phili

Sae

lake

clubs

KATE DE GOLDI

Jacqui Colley

REGISTER

1	Adele Gardener	✓	
2	Alexandra Bickerton	✓	
3	Alex McDonald	✓	
4	Bethany Griffiths	✓	
5	Billy Button ♯	✗	
6	Byron Bradshaw	✓	
7	Carla Patrikious	✓	
8	Danièlle Jellyman	✓	
9	Freddy Lafu	✓	
10	Georgie Piripi	✓	
11	Haami Weir	✓	
12	Jake Zwartz	✓	
13	Joseph Wojciechowski	✓	✳
14	Kendal Cummings	✓	
15	Lolly Leopold	✓	
16	Mary Etherington	✓	
17	Mika Malope	✓	
18	Neha Bava	✓	
19	Philimon Mbeki	✓	
20	Robert Rankin	✓	
21	Sam Van der Velde	✓	
22	Sae Gibbs	✓	
23	Tash Hirini Foster	✓	
24	Teuila Heffernan Tuuilalo	✓	

My teacher is a glorious creature.
She has a tuatara tattoo and a long ponytail that she swings like a lasso.
She says, 'WHAT'S THE STORY, GLORY?' and 'HEY IS FOR HORSES!' if we call out in class.
She smacks her hip and says, 'GIDDY UP FOLKS!' if we're dawdling.
She blows a long blast on her trumpet when we're getting down to work and shouts, 'OKAY, FOLKS, IT'S FLAT OUT LIKE LIZARDS DRINKING!'
She drives a Valiant Ranger, and a tough bargain.
My Dad says, Ms Love's one out of the box.

Ms Love says she'll play her trumpet at Grandparents' Day if I tell the Clubs story. She says it'll put smiles on all the grandparents' dials, or my real name's not Lorenza D. Leopold.
My real name IS Lorenza D. Leopold but you'd better call me Lolly, or there'll be big trouble.

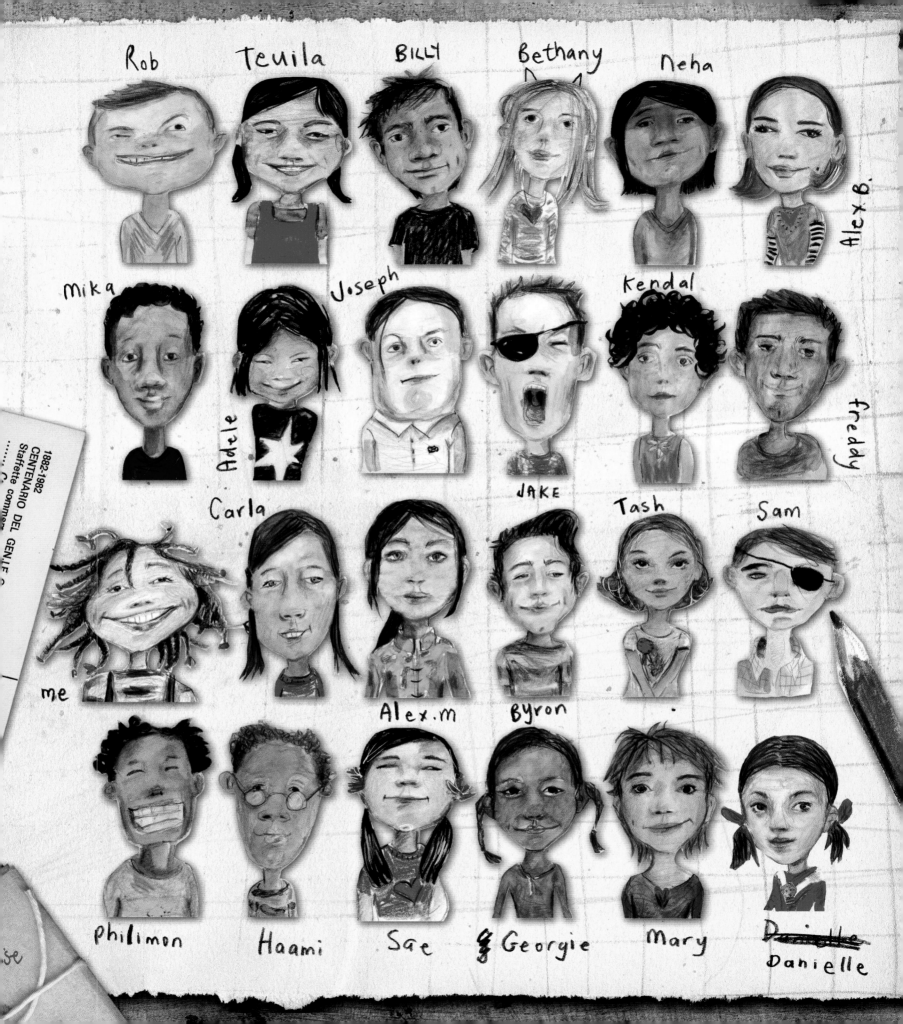

The clubs epidemic breaks out in March like a giant nit plague.
It spreads through our class 'til practically everyone's infected.
Not me. I must be inoculated.
First up is the Barbie Club. Bethany starts that. She has every Barbie
you can think of PLUS three Shave 'n' Style Kens. Bethany's house
is Barbie City 'cos her mother's been collecting them since ~~the~~ she
was zero.
Bethany's mother is a mean old Tartar. She said once, that if I was a
lolly it must be an Acid Drop.
Ms Love says, You have to admit that was witty.
My Dad says I really shouldn't have called her old Barbies
alien life forms.

Everyone in our class with a Barbie joins the Club, except me, even though I've got Totally Hair Barbie at home. The bad news is, now she's Practically Bald Barbie. My cousin, Barney Kettle, and I gave her a serious makeover. We shaved her and pierced her belly button and gave her a disease with a green felt pen. Then we glued her to my Dad's dinghy so she looked like a ship's figurehead.

My Dad says Barney Kettle and I share some ~~~~~ rogue gene.

The Barbie girls sit under the linden tree at lunchtimes with all their Barbies and Barbie outfits and Barbie accessories.

They hold Barbie Fashion Shows and Barbie Hair Conventions and Barbie Beach Cruiser Rallies. They have Barbie Beauty Contests too but Bethany's Barbies always win and vicious catfights erupt, so Ms Love has to Take A Stand. She declares herself a One Woman Barbie Beauty Contest Protest Movement and pickets them with a whistle and a placard until the contests are cancelled.

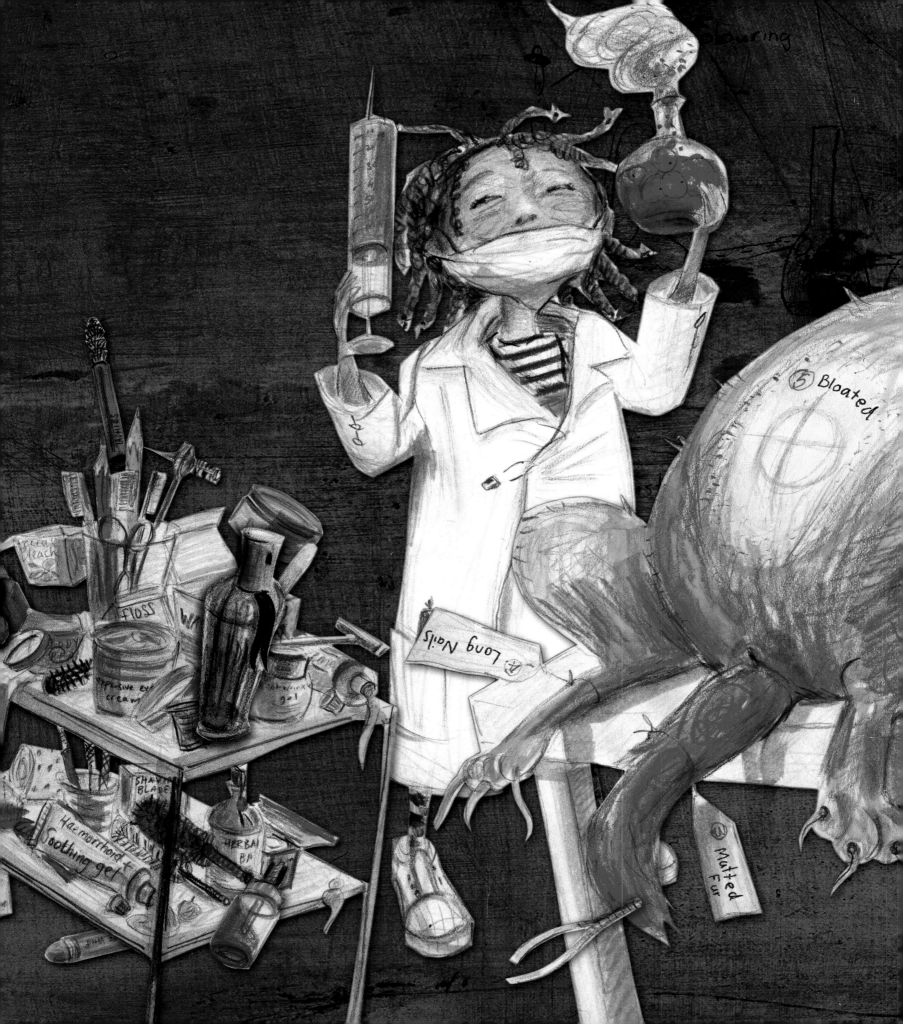

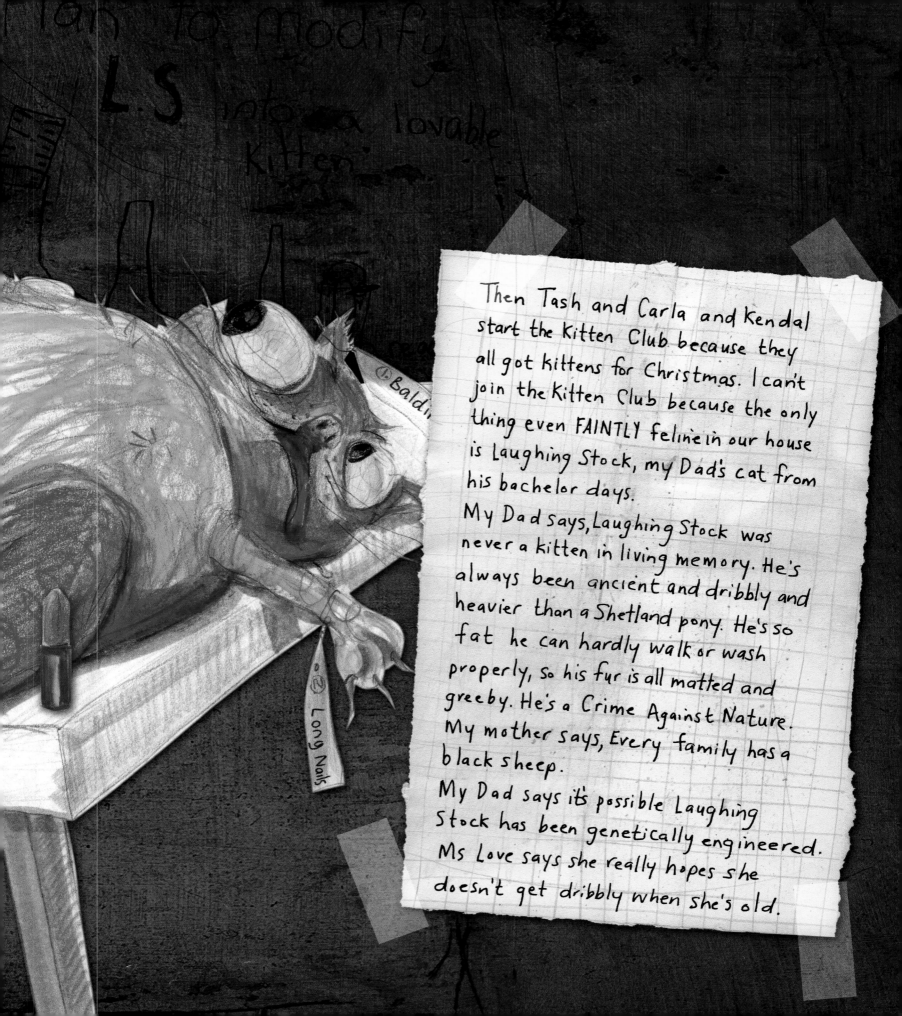

Then Tash and Carla and Kendal start the Kitten Club because they all got kittens for Christmas. I can't join the Kitten Club because the only thing even FAINTLY feline in our house is Laughing Stock, my Dad's cat from his bachelor days.

My Dad says, Laughing Stock was never a kitten in living memory. He's always been ancient and dribbly and heavier than a Shetland pony. He's so fat he can hardly walk or wash properly, so his fur is all matted and greeby. He's a Crime Against Nature.

My mother says, Every family has a black sheep.

My Dad says it's possible Laughing Stock has been genetically engineered.

Ms Love says she really hopes she doesn't get dribbly when she's old.

Mr De Luca, our Principal, says, NO WAY can kittens come to school, so the kitty girls just sing cat songs and make kitten badges and invent secret kitten passwords. They have a fancy notebook with The Miaow Rules written inside.

Those rules would freeze your blood. If you break a Miaow Rule you have to go to the corner of the playground and face the fence, but Tash cries all the way through Afternoon Reading when she has to do this, so Ms Love bans kitten Club punishments. She says members of Amnesty International have a duty to fight discrimination and torture.

knitted kittens
flying instructions
1. stuff kitten with light
   weight filler.
2. ___ kitten sky high
3. ___atch kitten when landing
4. sing kitty songs while kittens
   fly.

5. If kitten gets stuck on
   something high you can
   send another kitten
   up to rescue.
6. kittens cannot wear
   wings

My Dad says, The school playground is just like the business world. It's shark eat shark out there. I say, In that case, Tash better stay out of the business world because she's more nervous than a guppy.

Next thing, Jake starts the Lego Club. Lego is his LIFE. He has Rock Raiders in his desk and pirates in his pockets. He probably takes his Lego bricks to bed and I hope it hurts. Jake Zwartz and I have been enemies since pre-school. He keeps calling me Lorenza, so I have to keep putting unpleasant surprises in his backpack. Last year he called me Lorenza for an entire Thursday so I broke an old duck egg in his mailbox on the way to ~~steal~~ school.

The Lego Club assembles at 1230 hours on the steps outside our classroom. Their mission is building garrisons and battleships and launching pads, and then blowing them all sky-high.

They're so loud and violent that Ms Love sends a diplomatic envoy to their President. Naturally, Jake is President (he's Secretary and Chairman, too, but he makes Freddy Treasurer 'cos Freddy gets the most pocket-money). Ms Love says, Lower the decibels, Mr President. (She used to play in the Army Band, but now she's a Pacifist.)

peace
and quiet

torture chamber
residents

Bethany Griffiths
Mrs Lopdell (can't feed she bites)
Jake
Naomi W
Danielle Jellyman
Great Aunty Theckla.

DO NOT FEED SHE BITES

suush oool

I've got a bag of lego at home, but lego wars are strictly for pea-brains. I specialise in Lego castles with headless ghosts and battlements and staircases going nowhere. And a dark, stinking dungeon with a trapdoor as snappy as a crocodile's jaw.
My Dad says, Quite frankly, Lolly, there are worse places than a dungeon. [The living room apparently when I'm practising the piano.]

The fourth club is the Harry Potter Club. Haami starts this because he's a walking Harry encyclopedia and his house is bursting with Harry books and videos, Harry jigsaws, Harry writing paper, Harry games, you name it. The Junior wizards lurk behind The Fort waving their wands around and talking Harry code. They plot spells for dealing with Mrs Lopdell, the school secretary. Mrs Lopdell's been at school since prehistoric times. She is EXCEPTIONALLY grumpy. I wouldn't mind fixing her with some spell but the HP Club rules count me out. Rule **1**: you have to own all the Harry books [I do]. Rule **2**: you have to be a boy (#!!*!?@#!).

Ms Love says the Human Rights Commission would blast the HP Club out of the water, so they'd better keep their heads down.

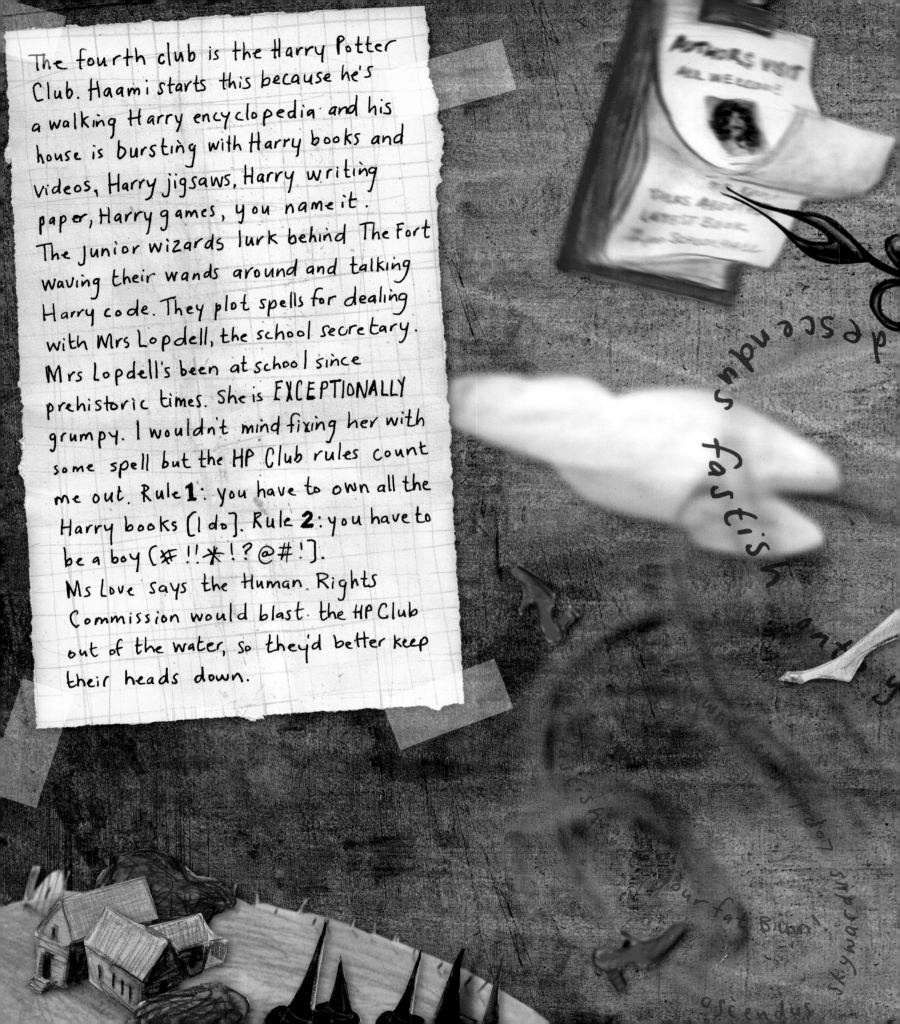

By the end of March there are only three people in Room 7 not in a club: me, Byron Bradshaw and Adele Gardner, the new girl from Brunei.

My mother says maybe I'd get into more clubs if I didn't leave surprises in people's mailboxes.

My Dad says pretty soon mailboxes will be a thing of the past.

At lunchtime when everyone's huddling in their club Byron comes over to The Fort. I'm hanging upside down listening in to the Harry Potter Club. 'You want to be in one of those clubs?' says Byron.

'I'd rather watch GRASS grow', I say. 'Same', he says. Byron Bradshaw is all right for a boy. He does great Elvis impersonations and he has the longest eyelashes in the school. Byron wants to know if Bethany's mother really did call me an Acid Drop. He wants to know if I've ever ridden a donkey. He wants to know if I've ever seen a person with a hooked hand. He wants to know what the D in my name stands for. [I'll never tell.] He asks so many questions I finally tell him to shut up, so he does, and he hangs upside down beside me.

Next thing, Adele is standing in front of us.
'What's up?' says Adele.
'We're watching grass grow,' we say at
EXACTLY THE SAME TIME.
'So this is the Grass Growing Club?' says
Adele.
'Don't be crazy,' I say. 'It's the Grass
Growing SPECTATORS' Club.'
'Yeah,' says Byron, 'you need acres of time
for this club, ha ha.'
'We've got a very exclusive membership,' I
say. 'You've got to have five letters in your
name to be eligible!'
'So eat grass!' says Adele, and she spells
the letters off on her fingers: A.D.E.L.E.

'And,' I say, 'you have to be able to say your name backwards without thinking!'

'Eleda Rendrag!' says Adele Gardner. 'Simple. I can do my whole family. Eleda, Mit, Nehpets, Esor and Nibor Rendrag. I've known THAT for years.'

I swing round the right way to get a good look at her. Only me and Barney Kettle have ever done backwards names straight off before.

'Hey!' I say, 'Eiram, Divad, Ecila, Revilo and Aznerol Dlopoel.'

Byron swings round too. 'Noryb, Nodrog, Noiram and Kram Wahsdarb!' he says.

It's one of those times when my Dad would say, 'KNOCK ME DOWN WITH A WET VOLE.'

'Move over,' I say to Byron, and Adele swings her leg over, too, and we all tip upside down and hang there like a trio of tree sloths.

And that's how the last club in Room 7 is formed. The Grass Growing Spectators' Club hangs out every lunchtime and always on The Fort.

And always upside down.

We like the view that way.

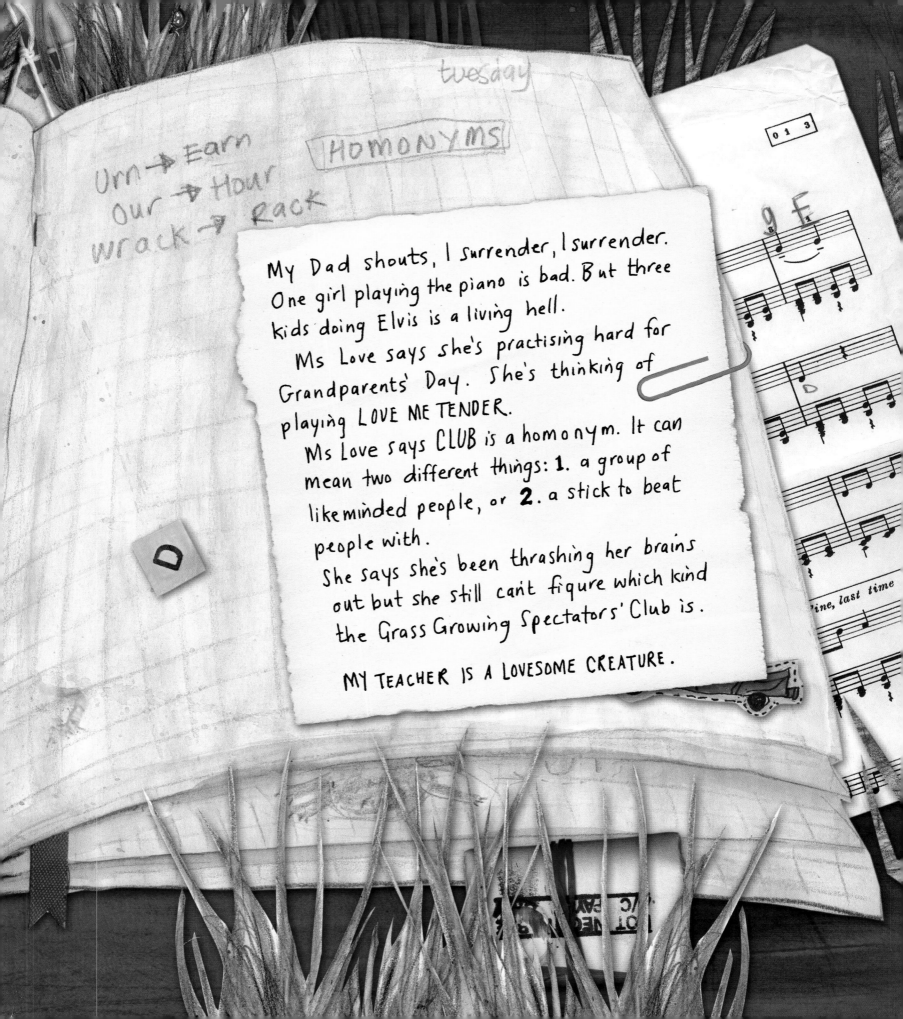

Urn → Earn
Our → Hour
Wrack → Rack

HOMONYMS

D

My Dad shouts, I surrender, I surrender. One girl playing the piano is bad. But three kids doing Elvis is a living hell.

Ms Love says she's practising hard for Grandparents' Day. She's thinking of playing LOVE ME TENDER.

Ms Love says CLUB is a homonym. It can mean two different things: **1.** a group of likeminded people, or **2.** a stick to beat people with.

She says she's been thrashing her brains out but she still can't figure which kind the Grass Growing Spectators' Club is.

MY TEACHER IS A LOVESOME CREATURE.

none nun

lknot not

leak leek

for

scene cent

Billy saw hair!

WAS

georgie
was here

1. Who was
2. Where is
3. What is
4. Your thou
Bull figh

Sae

Join

bubblegum
chocolate

Infinity CLUB
Go club
Titanic club
WHY?

desert island
① compass
② matches island

blo Picasso

olbap eht
tsitra

of the week

> chiaroscuro
> montage
> deconstruct
> abstractio
> minimalis

hts

ing?

(cent money)
scent
↑
stink

.com

Pjod.com

you stink

W.lolly.leo

you stink